To lovely Lottie (and Cloth and Rabbity). A.S.
For Maya, who will soon be big enough, too. L.M.

OXFORD
UNIVERSITY PRESS

Great Clarendon Street, Oxford OX2 6DP

Oxford University Press is a department of the University of Oxford.
It furthers the University's objective of excellence in research, scholarship,
and education by publishing worldwide in

Oxford New York

Auckland Cape Town Dar es Salaam Hong Kong Karachi
Kuala Lumpur Madrid Melbourne Mexico City Nairobi
New Delhi Shanghai Taipei Toronto

With offices in
Argentina Austria Brazil Chile Czech Republic France Greece
Guatemala Hungary Italy Japan Poland Portugal Singapore
South Korea Switzerland Thailand Turkey Ukraine Vietnam

Text copyright © Amber Stewart 2007
Illustrations copyright © Layn Marlow 2007

The moral rights of the author and artist have been asserted

Database right Oxford University Press (maker)

First published 2007

British Library Cataloguing in Publication Data available

ISBN-13: 978-0-19-279209-9 (hardback)
ISBN-10: 0-19-279209-1 (hardback)

ISBN-13: 978-0-19-279210-5 (paperback)
ISBN-10: 0-19-279210-5 (paperback)

10 9 8 7 6 5 4 3 2 1

Printed in China

Amber Stewart & Layn Marlow

I Love My Cloth

OXFORD
UNIVERSITY PRESS

Bean was big enough.

She was big enough to hop all the
way round Stickleback Pond
without stopping.

She was big enough to go dandelion
picking, to choose the juiciest ones
for Mummy to cook.

Bean was even big enough to swing
the highest of all her friends —
so high, her giggles could be heard
over and beyond Bluebell Wood,

so high, her tummy tumbled as up she flew.

She was big enough to do all these things, but was Bean big enough to stop taking Cloth just about everywhere she went?

'No,' said Bean. 'I love my Cloth.'

'Maybe you could try doing things without Cloth?'
said Mummy and Daddy gently.

'Yes — cloths are for babies,' said Bean's big brother.
'No they're not,' said Bean.

So Bean made a plan just in case her
family decided to take Cloth away.
She called it the 'keep Cloth forever plan'.

Early in the morning,
Bean set out to hide
Cloth in a secret place.

It wasn't on the edge of
Stickleback Pond because
the frogs might find it.

It wasn't between the branches
of Thunderstruck Tree because
the birds might take it.

It wasn't in the soft
earth because the voles
might want it.

Bean was just wondering if she would
ever find the right spot, when she saw a
hollow log hidden by overgrown brambles.

Bean hid Cloth deep in the hollow log —
and hurried home. She was happy all
day knowing that her Cloth was safe.

But when bedtime drew near, Bean wanted Cloth.
She had never ever had a bedtime without cuddling
Cloth, and she didn't want one now.

So Bean set out to her secret hiding place
to bring Cloth back home.

The wood looked different in the early evening light.
All the hollow logs seemed the same, and now
Bean wasn't sure which one

was her hiding place.

Was Cloth in that hollow log . . .

or that one . . .

or that one?

'Oh no!' cried Bean.
'My plan's gone wrong.
I've lost Cloth!'

Poor Bean had no choice but to turn for home.

Clothless, and close to tears, she saw Mummy.

'Bean, where did you go?' Mummy asked.
'To look for Cloth,' sniffed Bean, 'but I can't find it.'

Bean's family was very kind about the
lost-Cloth disaster.

Daddy read her two extra bedtime stories,
Mummy made her hot milk to help her sleep.
And Bean's brother lent her his
second-favourite teddy bear.

Bean didn't like her first
bedtime without Cloth.
She didn't much like
her second or
third either.

But soon looking for
Cloth turned into looking
for ladybirds and
four-leaf clovers . . .

and making the
very best dens . . .

and going hollow-log
sledging . . .

until Bean had forgotten all about her Cloth.

One windy spring day, a long time later,
Bean and her friends were chasing dandelion
clocks in a sunny part of the wood, when she
saw the strangest thing . . .

Bean looked at the tiny baby cub and knew
now that her Mummy was right —

she *really* was much too *big* for Cloth.